J   DeLaCro

Hero of

The Hero of Third Grade

The Hero of Third Grade

by Alice DeLaCroix

illustrated by
Cynthia Fisher

Holiday House / New York

Library of Congress Cataloging-in-Publication Data

DeLaCroix, Alice.
The hero of third grade / by Alice DeLaCroix; illustrated by Cynthia Fisher.—
1st ed.
p.   cm.
Summary: When Randall changes to a new school, he pretends
to be an anonymous hero until, when his third grade class
plans a fundraiser, he finds that being himself is good enough.
ISBN 0-8234-1745-X
[1. Self-confidence—Fiction.   2. Schools—Fiction.
3. Heroes—Fiction.   4. Carnivals—Fiction.]
I. Fisher, Cynthia, ill.   II. Title.

PZ7.D36965 He 2002
[Fic]—dc21   2002017123

For My Parents,
Ruby and Ermal Antrim:
She taught third grade heroes
He enjoyed her stories about them

Contents

Chapter 1
Mrs. Hubbard's Cupboard

His life was ruined. And Randall knew what had ruined it. Moving to a new town when school was nearly over. In April, no less! What could *be* worse than that?

Going back to his new school a second day. That's what.

Where NO ONE LIKED HIM, period, exclamation point.

He and his mother had moved here to Rushport right after the divorce. Dad stayed back in their old house, in their old town. And now Randall had this new school!

So here he was, getting ready for that second day. Ruined, ruined, ruined!

He took as long as he could to get dressed. His mother called every two seconds, "Randall, hurry. . . . Randall, I want you to have time for breakfast. . . . Randall, honey, hustle!"

The knots in his stomach didn't leave room for even one Oaty-o, anyway, she should know.

Before leaving his room he checked his rubber stamp collection. He slipped one stamp and an ink pad into his jeans pocket. Last night he had watched an old movie on TV with Mom about a guy called the Scarlet Pimpernel. It had put an idea in his head for how he might use the stamp.

The bus ride from their apartment to school was short. Too short. Dragging himself into school, Randall spotted Gordo with two of his friends. He saw a boy named Max just ahead of them. Next to himself, Max was the quietest kid in his third grade class, Randall thought.

Gordo, on the other hand, could make the teacher, Mrs. Hubbard, pull her hair,

Randall guessed already. His name was Gordon, and Mrs. Hubbard called him Gordon. But he wanted the kids to call him Gordo, so they did.

Their classroom was known as the Cupboard, because of an old Mother Hubbard nursery rhyme. Gordo had bragged yesterday to Randall that *he* had named it that. Randall doubted Gordo even knew any nursery rhymes.

But right now Gordo was boring down on Max. "Hey, Peanut!" he called. Then he bumped into Max, who was half his size. Papers fell to the floor. "Aw! Math homework," Gordo said. He flapped the paper in his friends' faces.

"Let me have it," Max said so softly Randall barely heard.

Gordo grinned. He wadded up the paper and tossed it over his shoulder. Then he and the others herded Max into the Cupboard, laughing.

The second they were out of sight, Randall scooped up the crumpled homework. This

was his chance! He smoothed it out as flat as he could. Then he stuck it in his folder.

He crouched against the hallway wall. Kids streamed by him. No one paid any attention as he wrote a note on a small scrap of paper:

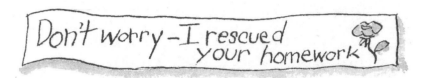

Then Randall sneaked his stamp and ink pad from his pocket. He carefully pressed a bright red flower onto the note. That's how the Scarlet Pimpernel had signed all his secret notes—an important fact Randall had learned last night.

The Scarlet Pimpernel did brave stuff a long time ago—like saving people from having their heads chopped off. Only in secret. Nobody knew who the Scarlet Pimpernel really was, but they went wild over him. So cool, Randall thought.

Aunt Wanda had sent Randall the stamp with the little roundish flower on it. She had seven girls. He guessed that was why she chose this one. He hadn't much liked it, but now it was perfect.

He folded the note into a small square. Then he walked on into the Cupboard, his stomach knots almost gone.

At Mrs. Hubbard's desk, Randall added his homework paper and Max's to the pile already started.

Now. How to get the note to Max without anyone seeing who it was from? Just then Gordo shoved past with his homework. He stepped right on Randall's toe. On purpose.

Randall bit his lip to keep in a Yow! But at the same time he saw that Max had left his desk. He had gone to sharpen one of his many pencils.

Randall forgot his toe and quickly walked by Max's desk. As he did, he passed his hand close over Max's open pencil box and dropped his folded-up note right in. Success!

A minute later, Max read the note and looked shyly around. Randall could tell Max really wondered who it was from. He grinned inside himself.

Chapter 2
A Pet What?

Being a secret hero got Randall through one more day of his first week in a new school. It didn't get him a friend, but he was somebody. He was the Scarlet Pimpernel. Sort of.

With his ink pad and flower stamp stored in his desk now, he kept a sharp eye and a keen ear out for other good, secret things he could do. That way Randall didn't think quite so much about how lonely he felt.

Mrs. Hubbard, with her smiling round face and blue sky eyes, wasn't old-Mrs.-Hubbardy at all, Randall had decided by the end of the week. "Class, what day is today?" she asked.

"Friday," some kids said.

Randall kept quiet.

"Go out and play ball day," Gordo said.

But most of the class answered, "Choose a tree day."

Lots of arms shot into the air. "I know. I know what tree I want!" several people shouted at once.

Mrs. Hubbard held her hand out, palm down so everyone would get quiet. "Now, you've all been looking around to find one special tree. One you can get to know very well. It will be your pet tree."

Randall could feel his blood pumping. His face was probably going red right that minute—so he really *was* scarlet. What tree? What was the teacher talking about? No one would like him if he didn't have a clue about things. He chewed his lip and tried to picture a tree, *any* tree around their apartment building.

Suddenly Mrs. Hubbard's voice broke through his haze. She was standing close by. "I'm sorry, Randall. I wrote this down on the

catch-up notes I sent home with you. But we talked in class about this before you came. Don't worry; there'll be a perfect tree for you. Tell me on Monday."

The catch-up papers. Randall knew he hadn't read all of them. But why would he even *want* a pet tree, he wondered? Everyone sure seemed excited about it, though. He smiled weakly. "Yes, ma'am," he choked out.

"Ma'am! He called her ma'am again," Gordo cried. Snickers spattered the room.

Randall could have torn out his tongue. Where he came from ma'am was just good manners. But somehow it wasn't right for here.

"Class. Settle," Mrs. Hubbard said. "Now let's go by rows, and I'll write in my book which tree each of you has chosen."

Michael wanted a big maple in his front yard. Caitlin chose an apple tree in her backyard. Walker named the huge old tree in the town square park as his choice.

"Oh, no! That's *my* tree," Tara claimed loudly.

"Mine, too," Dylan cried.

Randall watched, bewildered, as the class erupted in more shouts.

"She shouldn't have it. . . ." "That's the best tree. . . ." "Which tree?"

Mrs. Hubbard drew her eyebrows down and said, "What have we said about arguing?" She looked around at the biggest mouths—Randall was glad he wasn't one of them. "Okay. Remember the conditions we agreed on for your pet tree? Max, remind us, please."

Max said, "Everyone gets a different tree. And it has to be close to where you live."

"Now raise your hand if the biggest tree in the town park is your first choice."

Randall noticed that only Walker, Tara, and Dylan wanted that tree. Maybe he should put his hand up, too. He knew Rushport had trees, but no matter how hard he tried, he still couldn't picture a single one where he lived. Back in his old home there had been that tree he liked to climb, the one with scratchy bark. But he didn't want to think about that. There was some talk going on now, he realized, about who lived closest to the park.

"So Walker, you may have the biggest tree in the town park as your pet tree. You are three streets closer than anyone else," Mrs. Hubbard decided.

"Okay, we have about a hundred trees in our yard," Dylan said. "I'll take the biggest one."

"A hundred!" some kids scoffed.

"Bet he means a hundred stinkweeds in his yard," Gordo said.

But Tara let loose a wail that stopped everybody. She was crying.

Mrs. Hubbard gave her a chance to calm down. It wasn't until everyone else had named his or her tree—except Randall, of course—that Mrs. Hubbard came back for Tara's choice.

With one last huge sniff Tara said, "The tree . . . the tree next door. It sort of hangs over the fence."

"Not one in your own yard?" Mrs. Hubbard asked gently.

"Naw. They're all runty."

Randall liked the way Tara held her chin high when she said that. She had really wanted the biggest tree, which she'd had to give up. But she wasn't going to settle for a runty tree. He looked around to see that no one was watching him and then wrote a note to Tara:

Keep your chin up! Your tree will be better than the park one, I bet.

And signed it with his red flower stamp. The Scarlet Pimpernel.

Chapter 3
Who Wrote This?

At lunch that same day, Randall sat next to Max at the end of a table. It wasn't like anyone invited him. It was just a rule that classes had to sit together. In his old school they could sit anywhere they wanted. He had sat with his class anyway. Why not? He had lots of friends there.

He was about to bite into his PB&J when Tara started poking a little piece of paper in kids' faces. Randall thought he recognized it even from his end seat. His jaw was open, but he couldn't take a bite.

"Look at the note I got." Tara wasn't the

type to be ignored, so everyone looked. She read it out loud, then passed it along.

Randall was kind of pleased, kind of sick to his stomach. A glob of grape jelly leaked from his sandwich.

"I get notes all the time," Jenna said smugly.

"Yeah, but who's it from?" someone asked Tara.

"It's signed with a red flower."

"Yeah, a red daisy," said Dylan.

"Ha! Tara got a note from a daisy," Gordo yelled.

"You dopes, daisies aren't red," Walker declared. "My dad runs a garden nursery and I know."

Randall breathed a small sigh of relief. He didn't want to be known as some old *daisy.* Of any color!

"No, I know, I know!" said Caitlin. "I bet that's a scarlet pimpernel. You got a note from the Scarlet Pimpernel!"

"Huh?" everyone said.

Randall stuck his elbow in the jelly, but nobody saw. All eyes were still on Caitlin.

Caitlin sounded more excited with each word. "The Scarlet Pimpernel. Like the Broadway play. My aunt lives in New York and she took me to see it. And the movie was on TV last—"

"What's it mean?" Jenna interrupted, "The scarlet . . . whatever?"

"It's a little red flower," Caitlin went on. "And this really wonderful, romantic guy long ago signed all his secret notes that way."

Randall prayed his face didn't show all his feelings. Yes! he was thinking, because Caitlin was so right and now he could be known by the right name. Then, yikes: *romantic?* No, no. Brave. Daring and good. Not romantic!

"Oooh, Tara," Gordo said, making googly eyes.

"Ahhh, Tara," moaned Jenna.

"Shut up, you two. This note isn't romantic," Tara said.

"I didn't mean the *notes* were romantic," Caitlin explained in her teachy way, "just the guy. He helped people in trouble."

Randall couldn't stop a little smile from coming, so he finally took a quick bite of sandwich.

"Who wrote this? Did you?" Tara demanded, once more shoving the note at different kids along the table. She even passed it quickly by Randall. He just lowered his head and chewed a little harder.

Nobody tried to take credit for the note, so Tara folded it and put it in her pocket. She said, "Well, I think it's nice."

Max was saying something to him, Randall realized. "I got one of those notes," Max whispered. "Did you?"

"Me? Uh, n-no," Randall stammered. "Not yet." About ten chews later when he had control again, he asked, "What did yours say?" As if he didn't already know.

Chapter 4
The Scarlet Pimpernel to the Rescue

Saturday morning Randall decided to ask his mother about getting a pet tree. She was usually full of ideas.

"A tree," she repeated. "This is a small apartment for a tree, Randall. How about a fig tree?" She waved an arm toward her big house plant in the living room. "Or bonsai. That's a great idea, bonsai! They are plenty small enough to fit—"

Randall interrupted. "I kind of like that one in back of the building—the one with interesting gray bark." He had walked around Friday afternoon, looking for a tree, since there wasn't anyone to play with.

Mom raised her eyebrows. "Well, Randall. I doubt it will fit into your room." Her eyes twinkled.

Randall grinned. "Stop fooling around, Mom. I don't have to put it in my room. I just have to get to know all about it."

"Uh-huh," she said, as if that explained nothing. "Why this sudden interest in trees, honey?" She sipped from her coffee mug.

"Mo-om, didn't you read that stuff my teacher sent home? It tells all about it." Randall didn't let on that he hadn't read all of it himself until yesterday after school.

"Oh! Oh, gosh, there *was* something about pet trees; I remember now." She reached to squeeze Randall's shoulder. "I'm sorry, my brain is so full with the move, and getting you into your new school—"

"And your new job at the bank," Randall added. He understood that his mother was extra busy.

Mom smiled. "So tell me the details."

Randall explained how each member of the class had to choose his or her own pet tree. They would learn everything they could about it and share with the class after a lot of weeks—eight, he thought.

"Then we're going to send some trees to a school north of here, because they had a really bad ice storm and lost a bunch of trees," Randall explained all in a rush. He shrugged. "Does this make any sense?" he asked his mother.

"Possibly. As long as you don't have to dig up your pet tree to send," she said with a wink and a smile.

"I don't think so," Randall said. But he didn't know.

Randall helped his mother unpack the last of their moving boxes. That took some time. He had a good talk on the phone with his dad. That took some time. Mom and he went to Spaghetti Garage for dinner. But mostly, the weekend crept by.

Randall was almost glad when Monday and school came again. He thought of the flower stamp waiting in his desk. Then he felt brave enough to walk back into the Cupboard.

All morning Randall kept his eyes peeled for some good reason for a Scarlet Pimpernel note. Nothing showed up. Sometimes, he had to admit, he got involved in his real school work. Maybe he'd missed his chance.

But no. Right after recess when people were still getting drinks at the fountain, Randall slipped back to his seat. He wasn't hot and sweaty because he'd only *watched* kids playing kick ball. He raised the lid of his desk and pretended to be busy, even though he wasn't. Next thing Randall knew, he heard Gordo whisper and snigger with his buddies.

Randall peeked out and saw Gordo reach into Jenna's desk. Fast as a bird peck, Gordo snatched up Jenna's Beanie Baby. Then, sneaky as any snake, he tossed it behind a big "Life Cycle of a Tree" poster on the window ledge.

Randall gulped. He had seen it all.

When she got to her desk, Jenna let out a yelp. Her face turned almost purple when she cried, "Mrs. Hubaarrrd! Puffer is gone! Someone took my Beanie Baby!"

Mrs. Hubbard gave the class a little time for searching. The room was in a hubbub, so Randall managed to get a note written and drop it on Jenna's seat. He could have told

Mrs. Hubbard about Gordo. But that would be tattling, and nobody liked a tattler. The Scarlet Pimpernel could clear things up.

Jenna almost brushed the small square of white paper off her chair before sitting back down. Randall was glad she didn't.

"Hey. A note," she said, and opened it. Jenna shrieked. "It's from the Scarlet Pimpernel!" Randall didn't like the way she held her heart when she said that. Then she read his words out loud, "'Beanie Baby is behind tree poster. It is fine.' Signed with a red flower."

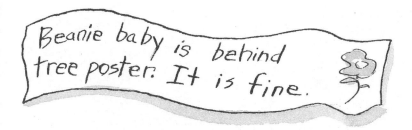

Mrs. Hubbard headed straight to the window ledge.

Gordo was already there. He peered around the poster. "Yep, it's here, all right." He held the puffin up by its beak.

Randall hated how proud of himself Gordo looked. He almost wished he could have just walked over and pulled out the toy himself. But that was impossible.

Jenna made an "ick" face when Gordo handed Puffer to her. As soon as the critter left Gordo's hands, she hugged it like a mom comforting a baby.

Gordo sneered back at her, but his eyes looked sad. Randall scratched his head. Gordo *liked* Jenna! That's why he'd hidden Puffer then found it.

Chapter 5
The Scarlet
Pimpernel Foiled

Tara passed out papers called My Tree Fact Sheets. Only they had to fill in the facts, Randall saw. When she got to him, Tara tapped his paper with her fingers, so he glanced up. Her dark eyes drilled him.

Did she know? Had she seen him drop the note to Jenna? His mouth went dry as a Texas gully. But then Tara gave him a big smile. A friendly smile, Randall thought. She moved on before he was over his shock enough to smile back.

Mrs. Hubbard explained, "In the next forty-five minutes each of you should make notes on your pet tree. Use the resources around the room. Eventually you will fill in all the blanks on this fact sheet. You'll know what leaf shape your tree has, what type of bark—"

"Woof! Woof, woof!" Gordo let out.

The class burst into laughter. Some of Gordo's buddies started a high "yip-yip-yip" and a low "rruff-rruff-rruff." Others joined in. Mrs. Hubbard got things in control again just in time. Randall had felt a little "yap" scratching at the back of his own throat.

When everyone moved to the resource areas, Randall sat rooted. The teacher had stuff all around—books, pictures, charts, lots of things—but if Randall got up he'd have to join some group of other kids. Who would want a new kid butting in?

"Randall, why don't you begin at the computer?" Mrs. Hubbard suggested. He picked up his notebook and started toward the computer in the corner. "See what you can find on the Internet," she said.

Eeep! The Internet?! There had been a computer lab in his old school. He was sure there hadn't been an Internet.

"Max, I'd like you to work with Randall. Okay?"

Both Max and Randall gave quick nods of their heads.

Randall was surprised how easy it was, once Max showed him how to use the Internet. He was surprised how easy it was to feel less "new" around Max, too.

"Look, there!" Randall said. "I think that's a lot like my tree. It's hard to be sure since it doesn't have leaves yet, but it's got that kind of bark."

"Then it might be a beech. Like mine," Max said. "You started your diary?" He stretched out the word and made it funny. Max's ears went up when he grinned, Randall noticed.

Randall rolled his eyes. "Diary," he repeated, and they both laughed. "Yeah, yesterday. Not much going on yet—a squirrel ran up it," he said. They were to keep a diary on their pet tree's days. Since it was spring, things were supposed to be happening.

"I named my tree Ali Baba," Max said quietly.

"Like Ali Baba and the Forty Thieves?" Randall said.

"You know that story?" Max asked, pleased.

"It's cool," said Randall.

"Yeah," Max agreed. His ears went up.

Randall said then, "I'm thinking I will name mine General."

"That's good. General who? General Patton the great tank commander, General Lee—"

"Just General," Randall decided on the spot. He could see that Max knew lots of things in his quiet way. Randall liked that.

When everyone had returned to their seats, Mrs. Hubbard said, "Class, you had a very successful bake sale for Valentine's Day. We have a bit more than half the money we need to buy the trees for Morton Elementary School."

Buy trees. That settled the digging-up business Mom had gotten Randall worried about. He sure hadn't believed that would happen, but sometimes grown-ups still surprised him.

"Now we need ideas for a second fundraiser. Something we all can take part in."

Caitlin's hand went up, and a couple of others.

But Mrs. Hubbard went on. "I want each of you to put on your thinking cap and then write down your suggestion. I'll collect them and we'll vote on the best fund-raiser idea. Please put your name on your paper."

Randall knew what would be good. It just sprang into his head. A carnival! Everyone could be part of an act. There would be all sorts of fun things to do.

But . . .

But no. The kids would never choose *his* idea, no matter how good it was. He just wasn't part of the class. He wanted so much to turn it in signed "the Scarlet Pimpernel."

He chewed his lip, looking around. Next thing, he had his desk lid up, just enough to slip his hand in. His fingers reached the rubber stamp.

Oh no. Tara was watching him. She looked real suspicious.

There was just no way to write a Scarlet Pimpernel note when everyone was sitting quietly at their desks. He turned in his idea signed "Randall." Too bad. A carnival really was a great idea, he thought, sighing, but he knew it would never be chosen.

Chapter 6
Who *Is* the Secret Hero?

The next morning Mrs. Hubbard began class with the fund-raiser vote. She said, "I sorted your suggestions last night. There were some terrific ones, but I don't think 'rob a bank' counts." She let the class laugh at that.

"There were a number of suggestions for a second bake sale. I'm sorry I failed to say yesterday that we would do better not to repeat the same activity. I think we could include a bake sale along with another activity, though." Mrs. Hubbard passed a kind look over the class.

She continued, "Without another bake sale and the bank hold-up, we have three ideas to choose from. Several of you thought of a car wash, a few of selling greeting cards, and one of a carnival." She turned and wrote on the board: Car Wash, Sell Greeting Cards, Carnival.

"Oooh, a carnival," Jenna said, twirling her long ponytail.

"Oh, oh, oh!" Tara said. "I know what I could do in the carnival."

"Let's have a little discussion on each idea before voting," said the teacher.

"Older kids are always having car washes," Caitlin said. "We should do something different."

"Well, cars are neat," Dylan said, "and they always need washing."

"Bor-ing," groaned Tara. "I could do a tumbling act in a carnival."

"That's what *I* was going to say," Jenna snapped.

After allowing a few more minutes for the class to consider a car wash and card sales, Mrs. Hubbard said, "Randall, perhaps you could explain your carnival idea."

Randall couldn't believe his ears. How could she ask him to do that? It felt like an elephant had sat on his chest. He panted for breath and tried to speak. "We—we—we—" he started.

"Wee, wee, wee, all the way home!" Gordo shouted. Everyone hooted.

"Cut it out," Mrs. Hubbard demanded.

Randall felt faint. He *couldn't* pass out—could he? He held his head.

"A carnival would be super. Tell us, Randall," came a voice. Tara's, he thought.

He stared ahead. I am the Scarlet Pimpernel—I do brave things, he told himself. The elephant vanished, and Randall's mouth opened. He wouldn't start with "we" this time, though. "Our class could invite all the school kids and parents. It could be on a Saturday, maybe in the gym. Everyone could do something. . . ." He began to actually hear himself talking and dwindled off. But by then other people jumped in with more ideas. They sounded excited.

Randall began to hope.

"Thank you, children," the teacher said. "It is time to vote."

When the vote was taken, a lot of boys chose the car wash. But there were more girls in the class than boys, and most of them had been swayed to choose the carnival. Max voted for the carnival, Randall saw. And so did Gordo!

Randall blinked. His idea had won!

"Okay," Mrs. Hubbard said. "We have our work cut out for us, but a carnival should be a good moneymaker."

"And FUN!" more than one person said.

Mrs. Hubbard smiled. "I'll make the arrangements for the gym. What acts or booths shall we have?" She listed things on the board as different kids told what they wanted to do. Tara: tumbling; Jenna: tumbling; Michael: fortune-telling swami.

"Can we bring animals?" Gordo asked, wiggling in his seat. "We can, can't we, 'cause I've got my monkey. People will like him. That's the only reason I voted for this thing."

"A monkey!"

"You got a monkey, no fooling?"

"You're the monkey!"

"Am not. And I do have. His name's Slick." Gordo glared around the room defiantly. "He's fast and kind of sneaky."

"You would have to keep him in control," Mrs. Hubbard warned.

"Oh, yeah. I got a leash. And Slick's good, really. I promise."

A live monkey could attract a lot of customers, Randall thought.

Caitlin spoke up. "Then can I bring my Pomeranian, Lilly? She walks on her hind legs and does flips. She'd make a fabulous act."

"How does, uh, Slick get along with small dogs, Gordon?" Mrs. Hubbard ventured to ask.

Gordo shook his head all around—more in a circle than a real up-and-down yes or side-to-side no. "No problém-o. I promise."

"Well, I suppose we can have the dog and monkey on opposite ends of the gym." The teacher wore a small frown as she wrote down Caitlin: dog tricks.

Then Max surprised Randall by saying, "I can do a magic act." Who would have guessed?

Someone else had a clown outfit from Halloween. And so it went until there was quite a list in almost no time.

Before he knew what he was doing, Randall raised his own hand. Then he was saying right out, "I could bring my ring toss game. It's hard to win. I'd need some prizes for anyone who did win, though." He and his dad had built a super ring toss last fall. He'd like the chance to use it.

"I have a special catalog," said Mrs. Hubbard. "We can order some small prizes very cheaply, and pay back our class budget after the carnival."

Randall thought that sounded great. He was feeling pretty good about things. Then right after lunch, Jenna let out a shriek that put her lost-Puffer scream to shame.

"A note. I got another note from the Scarlet Pimpernel," she shouted. " 'Your cute!!' " she read for everyone to hear, even read the exclamation points. Her cheeks were pink with joy.

Randall sucked in air. What? he thought, I didn't write a note.

"Hold on, hold on!" Tara was saying as she snatched the note from Jenna. "This is bogus. It isn't from the Scarlet Pimpernel."

"Is too," Jenna insisted. "You're just jealous—"

"No! Look. Somebody drew that flower with marker."

Caitlin nosed in, too. "And 'your' is wrong," she said. "It should be y-o-u apostrophe r-e."

"Gordo"—Tara turned a glare on him like a searchlight—"that's your writing."

"Gordo? Eeuu!" fussed Jenna.

Tara went on, "Gordo, you are not the Scarlet Pimpernel."

"Says you," Gordo responded. He pulled a wet lump of paper from his mouth, then flipped the spit-wad at Tara.

Randall started breathing again. Thank you, oh thank you, Tara, he thought. The Scarlet Pimpernel would *never* write a sickening note like that. *Your cute*—ugh!

Now people were wondering more than ever who the Scarlet Pimpernel was, Randall bet. He had to bite his cheeks to keep from grinning.

Chapter 7
In the Game at Last

Randall walked into the Cupboard the next day right beside Max. Just last night when she'd tucked him in, Mom had said he might see if Max would come over to play soon. "Hey," Randall asked now, "where do you live? I didn't see what bus you ride."

"My mom is school secretary. I come with her," Max told him.

Gordo pushed between Randall and Max, saying, "Why don't you make like a tree and leave?" He haw-hawed at his own joke.

Somebody should teach him some manners, Randall thought. But he sure didn't have the nerve. He didn't even have the nerve to ask if Max's mom might drive him to his apartment sometime. Max might not want to come.

Randall aimed for his desk without saying another word.

Later he was glad that when the class did tree work, he and Max got together. They compared their diaries.

"'Ali Baba is getting tiny new leaves,'" Max read.

"General is, too," Randall said. "But the branches are too high. I can't see what shape they'll be."

"Nope. Me either," Max agreed. "I still think mine's going to be a beech tree."

Randall nodded. "Mine, too. There must be lots of beech trees around here."

It seemed all of them were pretty excited about their own trees.

Randall heard Caitlin boasting that her tree had bunches of white blossoms.

"That's nothing," Dylan said. "My tree has compound leaves. And they're already out full."

"Aw, that's *really* nothing," Gordo boomed out, "my tree got peed on today by a Saint Bernard."

Randall found himself laughing along with everyone else. Even though Mrs. Hubbard frowned.

On the playground in the afternoon, Tara surprised Randall by grabbing his arm and tugging him along. She was pulling him into the kick ball game, he realized. "You can be on my team," she said.

In the game at last! Randall thought, taking a stance, ready for the ball. He knew he was grinning like a dope, but he couldn't help it.

Then Tara nudged his shoulder and asked, "Who do you think the Scarlet Pimpernel is?"

"Uh, I don't . . . I don't know kids very well," Randall said. That wasn't a lie, like saying "I don't know" would have been. He felt his heart do a fast step. He was hoping she didn't ask him point-blank if he was the Scarlet Pimpernel.

But all Tara said was, "Well, I'm going to find out." Her eyes snapped and she kicked the ball hard.

Randall was so glad to be in the game, he tried his best. He was rusty, but still he got in some good kicks. At the same time he tried to decide if he wanted to be found out or not. Right now it was fun being the only one who knew who the Scarlet Pimpernel was.

Besides, everyone seemed to like the secret note-sender, even if most of the class still paid no attention to Randall. Why would he want to give that up?

After playground Mrs. Hubbard read some poems about trees. "I think that I shall never see, a poem as lovely as a tree" rang in Randall's head as he tried to write a poem about his tree. General was a good tree. But Randall slipped from tree poems to thinking about the carnival. It was four whole weeks away.

Four weeks usually seemed a very long time. But with all the preparations for the carnival, those days flew by.

During announcements each morning of the final week, Caitlin reminded the whole school to come to the carnival Saturday, May 19th.

Randall drew posters and hung them in the school entryway. FUN! CRAZY FUN! CARNIVAL FUN! he wrote. He hoped enough people came. He sure didn't want the carnival to be a big flop, since it was his idea.

There was so much going on in the Cupboard, Randall barely had time to think about the Scarlet Pimpernel. It was hard being a secret watcher/helper when you were right in the middle of things. But when he did find three more chances to write notes, he tried to disguise his writing each time. That Tara was checking.

And then it was carnival day.

Chapter 8
Monkey Business

"Look at this!" said Randall's mom when they entered the school gym together. "Wow! I'm impressed."

Randall beamed. "Yeah, it's okay." Mrs. Hubbard and the class, plus several parents, had spent time after school yesterday setting things up. With finishing touches this morning, all was ready.

Max wore a dark suit jacket with the tip of a red silk handkerchief showing from the pocket. He waved his black wand at Randall. "I'm kind of nervous," he said.

"You'll be great," Randall told him. "Do a

warm-up trick for me. The doors don't open yet."

"Okay." Max took a deep breath. "Okay," he said again, smoothing his hair. Then he dazzled Randall and his mother with a flying coin trick.

Mom clapped.

Randall said, "How'd you do that?"

"Magic!" Max said, and grinned so that his ears went up.

Jenna and Tara were poised on their tumbling mat. Jenna wore pink tights; Tara, purple. Nearby Tara's little sister waited to turn on their boom box music at the right moment.

Across the way Caitlin was trying to control her dog. The Pomeranian was barking and baring little pointy teeth at people. Yikes, Randall thought. Maybe that act was going to bomb.

Cupcakes, brownies, and lots of other baked goodies for sale were displayed on a table. One of the girls and her father were in charge there.

Bright balloons decorated booths. Good smells started drifting as one class member popped corn. Walker set out trays of candy apples he had brought from home. The orange-wigged clown stalked by on short stilts.

Yep, it was a carnival, all right, Randall decided. A strange feeling spread through him, as if he'd just grown an inch or two taller. For the first time since he'd moved here he felt sure of himself. Just the way he used to.

Then Randall spotted Gordo at the far end of the room. A crowd of third graders had already swarmed around him and Slick.

Randall poked Max. "See Gordo's monkey? Sitting on his shoulder?"

"Neat outfit," Randall's mother said.

"Yeah," Randall agreed. Slick wore a yellow vest with pockets outlined in some kind of sparkles. Pretty fancy.

Max said what Randall had been thinking, "Sure hope that monkey behaves better than Gordo does."

Finally the doors were opened. People flooded in. Everyone stopped to pay the entrance fee at a card table skirted in white fabric with photos of trees fastened to it. Mrs. Hubbard put the money into a gold-colored box with a flip lid.

Randall's Ring Toss was set up first thing after the pay table.

"Want me to be your first customer?" his mother asked.

"Okay," Randall said.

But right then a little boy stopped at his spot. "I want to play," he said boldly.

"I'll go look at the other booths and be back," Mom said.

"Sure," Randall said. "Step right up," he told the boy. He called out like a real carnival barker, "Step right up! Try your luck! Score twenty points and win a fabulous prize!" He had a stash of tiny plastic figures and toys that Mrs. Hubbard had helped him order for prizes. And before he knew it there were two more kids waiting their turn to play.

Time passed quickly for Randall because he was having fun. Laughter and happy babble all around made him feel that others were, too.

The gym was crammed with people. Whole families had come, even grandparents. Every now and then some would leave, but others would take their places. By the second hour Randall bet they had already made enough money to buy their trees. It looked like Mrs. Hubbard needed a bigger cash box—a stack of bills was pushing up the hinged lid.

Then, in seconds, everything turned topsy-turvy.

"Uh, oh!" Randall said to himself as he saw Caitlin's dog dart across the floor. It was aimed toward Gordo's end of the gym.

Caitlin scrambled after her, calling, "Lilly! Lilly, come back!" But in a moment the furry streak was lost in the crowd.

Then shrieks and screams. And an unearthly animal sound Randall had never heard in his life.

Slick was loose, too! Slick was bounding over people, springing from bald head to shoulder to curly head. "Eeek!" "Yow!" "Yiii!"

"Hey, look!" The monkey hung by his tail on the basketball hoop. Then in the next moment, he dropped from sight.

Mrs. Hubbard charged past Randall. She was rushing toward Gordo, but Slick was already far from there. He was on the move!

"There he is!"

"Catch him!"

"Where?"

Suddenly Slick appeared, zipping along with the Pomeranian nipping at his heels.

As Lilly cut across the tumbling mat, Jenna threw a well-timed block. She and Tara held the wriggling bundle down until Caitlin scooped her up.

Then there was a *bump* that caused Randall to look toward the pay table. He saw a monkey paw slip beneath the tablecloth, which hung to the floor.

Hah, Randall thought, I've got you now. But he stopped in his tracks when he noticed something even worse than a runaway monkey.

The lid to the cash box was wide open. At least half the bills were gone!

Chapter 9
A Hero for Real

"Max!" Randall cried.

"What?" Max scurried over from his magic booth.

"Look!" Randall pointed to the box.

"Oh, no! Who stole our money?"

"Keep your eye on that box," Randall ordered. Then he ducked under the table. He banged into a table leg. The table wobbled like a top on its last spin.

"Hey! What's going on under there?" he heard Max ask, but he couldn't answer.

He eyed Slick. Slick eyed him. "Come here, boy," he coaxed. For a split second Randall wondered if monkeys bite, then lunged. And missed.

With a shriek, Slick scooted away, about to escape, but got caught up in the table-cloth.

Randall snatched Slick by his vest, untangled him from the fabric, and crawled out. "Got you!" he said.

"Oh, wow!" said Max.

Slick clung to Randall's shirt with his little hands. His eyes were big as moons.

Randall straightened Slick's yellow vest and patted him to calm him. In that short moment he also made a choice—about the wad of money he'd seen in Slick's fancy pocket, the class money, no doubt. He decided not to say anything for the time being.

Then with a nod to Max, the two of them shouted, "Gordooo!"

Gordo and Mrs. Hubbard and half the gym full of people came trotting.

Gordo was sweating from chasing around the gym, hunting Slick, and his face was puckered with worry. "Get over here, Slick," he growled. The monkey leaped into Gordo's arms.

"Now where is that leash you were supposed to have?" Mrs. Hubbard asked, panting.

"Sorry," Gordo mumbled. "But Slick didn't need it at all. Until that wild dog attacked him."

"Yeah," Dylan said from the group crowded around. "Caitlin's dog ran right up to poor old Slick and bit his tail. Guess it got bored with rolling over and playing dead."

Several people laughed. Mrs. Hubbard grimaced. Caitlin made a lame excuse for Lilly, but no one really listened.

Tara pushed her way next to Randall. "You caught Slick!" she shouted for everyone to hear. "You're our hero!" She grabbed his arm and held it up like a winner.

"Hero, hero!" others joined in.

Randall felt his face blush red, but he smiled the widest smile he had in him. He was a hero being just plain Randall.

Standing in the crowd, Randall's mother caught his eye and gave him a big wink.

Mrs. Hubbard thanked him, then told everyone, "We still have twenty minutes left. Let's get the show going again. We promised people a carnival."

Randall walked back to the pay table with Mrs. Hubbard. Max still guarded the half-empty box.

"Someone took a bunch of our money, Mrs. Hubbard," said Max.

"Oh, my! All the confusion . . . Oh, I shouldn't have left it."

"Randall had me guard the rest of it," Max explained.

Then the teacher looked at Randall, a question in her eyes. "Randall, you were closest. Did you see who took it?" she asked.

"No, ma'am. I was looking the other way." Did she suspect *him*? He swallowed and turned from her. He did know who took the money. The question was, would it be turned in, or kept? Randall would tell if he had to, without using a secret note. But he wanted to give Gordo a chance first.

"Mrs. Hubbard!" squalled Gordo. He was stomping toward her. Slick still had his arms wrapped around his neck. Gordo looked mad.

"What now, Gordon?" asked the teacher. She pushed damp hair from her eyes.

Randall was relieved to hear what he said.

"Look. Look what I found in Slick's pocket."

"Oh, Gordon. The class money. Thank you. I didn't know how we would find the thief."

One of Gordo's buddies snickered and said, "Cool, Gordo, teaching your monkey to take money."

Gordo poked him with his elbow. "I did not! He just likes to stuff his pockets. Well, Mrs. Hubbard? It's all right, isn't it?" Gordo asked, his mouth saggy.

Mrs. Hubbard's bright white teeth showed with her grin. "It's all right. Everything's all right." She gave Gordo and Randall each a pat on the back.

Randall was glad Gordo hadn't made him tell on Slick. This carnival had been more exciting than Randall had ever imagined. And the best day he had had in his new school, that was for sure.

Chapter 10
General Ali Baba

Two more weeks brought the end of May. In that time several good things had happened.

First Tara had cornered Randall a few days after the carnival. "It's too weird," she said. "All at once we have a Scarlet Pimpernel in our class. Then all at once we *don't* have a Scarlet Pimpernel." She stuck her face close to his. "Why do ya think, Randall?"

"Maybe he isn't needed anymore, Tara," Randall answered. He was kind of surprised himself. The Scarlet Pimpernel had been so important to him. Being a secret, brave guy was exactly what he needed when he first came here. But now he almost never thought of him. Now he was happy just being himself. Of course, it helped that he was still a hero.

"Okay," Tara said and gave him one of her x-ray looks. "But I kind of miss your-uh-his notes," she said and whacked his arm.

Randall just shrugged elaborately. Maybe he would write her a note signed with a little red flower *and* his name. Or maybe not.

Second, the entire class had gone on a field trip to Walker's parents' nursery. There amid bright spring flowers and potted bushes and baby trees, they had selected their gift.

They chose two sugar maples and three crab apple trees.

Walker's father was to deliver the trees in his big landscape truck. Everyone agreed that Walker should go with him to present the trees.

Afterward Mrs. Hubbard had said, "See, class?" She held up a big photo. It showed the third grade class at Morton Elementary school accepting the trees from Walker and his dad. "All your planning and hard work and fun turned out beautifully."

Randall sat straight and tall. Everyone in the Cupboard beamed satisfied looks.

Last of all, it was time for the class to hand in their folders of tree work: science facts, poems, diaries, photos and drawings of their pet trees, interviews of people who knew their pet trees, everything they had worked on since Randall had come to his new school.

"We've done a lot of sharing through the weeks," Mrs. Hubbard said. "Now I would like each of you to tell the one most interesting thing you discovered about your pet tree."

Max raised his hand high. "Mrs. Hubbard, the *most* interesting thing I've learned is that my tree is the same tree as Randall's."

"Oh, my. How did that happen?" the teacher wondered.

"We didn't know," said Max. "We didn't even know we lived in the same apartment

complex." He turned a smile on Randall that made his ears go up about as far as they could possibly go.

Randall nodded his head happily.

And on the way out of school that afternoon Max called to Randall. "Meet me under General Ali Baba after your dinner."

"Sure. Under General Ali Baba," Randall agreed.

He could hardly wait.